C2 000003 283 509 XE

D1363208

Hey, Steve!

Yeah, Steve?

You know your hamster, Cuddly Jim?

What about him?

Well, just imagine if he got mangled by a cat.

Eurgh! That'd be horrible…

And then some mad scientist, who's discovered Dr Frankenstein's notebook, comes along and brings Cuddly Jim back to life.

That'd be great.

No it wouldn't, not if it was Vernon Bright who did it.

Why not?

Cos cuddly Jim wouldn't be cuddly any more.

Wouldn't he?

No, not if Vernie did to him what he did to Mister Nibbles the school hamster.

What did he do to Mister Nibbles?

You'll have to read the book and find out.

About the authors

Steve Barlow is tall and hairy. Steve Skidmore isn't.

They have written quite a few books together. Barlow does the vowels, Skidmore does the consonants. They generally leave the punctuation to sort itself out. They like writing, especially when it gets them out of doing the shopping, the ironing or the washing up.

Their other Puffin books include the *Mad Myths* series, which they say is fast, furious, fantastic and frightfully silly.

You can find out more about Steve Barlow and Steve Skidmore on the Web. Visit them at www.puffin.co.uk

Some other books by
Steve Barlow and Steve Skidmore

VERNON BRIGHT AND
THE MAGNETIC BANANA

VERNON BRIGHT AND
THE FASTER-THAN-LIGHT SHOW

MAD MYTHS: STONE ME!
MAD MYTHS: MIND THE DOOR!
MAD MYTHS: A TOUCH OF WIND!
MAD MYTHS: MUST FLY!

STEVE BARLOW AND STEVE SKIDMORE

Vernon Bright and

FRANKENSTEIN'S HAMSTER

Illustrated by
GEO PARKIN

PUFFIN BOOKS

PUFFIN BOOKS

Penguin Books Ltd, 27 Wrights Lane, London W8 5TZ, England
Penguin Putnam Inc., 375 Hudson Street, New York, New York 10014, USA
Penguin Books Australia Ltd, Ringwood, Victoria, Australia
Penguin Books Canada Ltd, 10 Alcorn Avenue, Toronto, Ontario, Canada M4V 3B2
Penguin Books India (P) Ltd, 11 Community Centre, Panchsheel Park, New Delhi – 110 017, India
Penguin Books (NZ) Ltd, Cnr Rosedale and Airborne Roads, Albany, Auckland, New Zealand
Penguin Books (South Africa) (Pty) Ltd, 5 Watkins Street, Denver Ext 4,
Johannesburg 2094, South Africa

On the World Wide Web at: www.penguin.com

Penguin Books Ltd, Registered Offices: Harmondsworth, Middlesex, England

First published 2000
3

Text copyright © Steve Barlow and Steve Skidmore, 2000
Illustrations copyright © Geo Parkin, 2000
All rights reserved

The moral right of the author and illustrator has been asserted

Set in 12½/18 Palatino

Made and printed in England by Clays Ltd, St Ives plc

Except in the United States of America, this book is sold subject to the condition that it
shall not, by way of trade or otherwise, be lent, re-sold, hired out, or otherwise circulated
without the publisher's prior consent in any form of binding or cover other than that in
which it is published and without a similar condition including
this condition being imposed on the subsequent purchaser

British Library Cataloguing in Publication Data
A CIP catalogue record for this book is available from the British Library

ISBN 0–141–30585–1

BIRMINGHAM LIBRARIES
J
SHELDON

CONTENTS

The two Steves would like to thank Trevor Day for his invaluable advice on the scientific principles referred to in this book, and for pointing out which of our ideas were 'come on, boys, that's totally impossible' and which were merely 'completely gaga, but what the heck, it's sci-fi.' Any remaining inaccuracies are what we managed to slip in while he was looking the other way.

The writing of this book was closely monitored by the RSPCA at all times. The two Steves wish it to be known that absolutely no hamsters were injured or ill-treated in the production of this book.

CHAPTER ONE

A Knife in the Kidneys

'Your kidneys are dripping.'

'Well, so are yours.'

'No, they're not. I've got mine in a plastic container.'

John Watt gulped and stared straight ahead. The rest of the class chattered happily as they waited to be let into the lab.

'Oh no! My kidney's dribbled all over my history homework.'

'I put mine in my lunchbox.'

'Gross!'

'Only kidding. I put it in my pencil case really.'

John's next lesson was with Ms Session, a biology teacher of the old school. She believed in the 'hands on' approach. She sometimes made her students put their hands on things that gave John the heebie-jeebies.

This week, they were dissecting kidneys. The previous week's homework had been to find some nice fresh kidneys and bring them in to the next session. Many of the waiting students were carrying cold, squishy parcels. Down the line from John, a couple of boys were using their plastic bags for an impromptu game of kidney-conkers.

John was already feeling a bit light-headed. He hated dealing with anything that belonged out of sight inside something's skin. He only had to open his biology textbook to start feeling nauseous. He hadn't brought a kidney to the class, but that was all right because his friend Vernon Bright had brought several. Of course, Bright wasn't carrying kidneys in a plastic bag. He was cradling in his arms a heavily insulated container made of high-impact plastic, which he said would keep the kidneys at a constant 3° Celsius until they were needed.

'It stops tissue from decomposing quickly,' he had told John on the way to school that morning.

'You don't want your kidneys to shrivel up, do you?'

Bright did things like this because he was a scientific genius, as he would be the first to admit. He was good at a lot of things, but modesty wasn't one of them. His dad did something with the Intelligence Services – his job seemed to be mostly to do with finding new ways of blowing up the world – which kept him away from home a lot. This meant that Bright had the run of the state-of-the-art mad-scientist's laboratory his dad had installed in the cellar. He spent most of his free time down there, doing experiments.

The kidney-conker match ended when the plastic bag belonging to one of the combatants split, and an unspeakable lump of crimson wobbliness shot out and slapped wetly on to the floor.

John clapped his hand to his mouth and staggered groggily towards the nearest toilet.

'Gangway!' shouted one of the conker players. 'Puke alert! Sicko coming through!'

By the time John had emerged from the toilet, feeling slightly better, the class had been allowed into the lab. People were working in groups of three. Each group had one or two kidneys, a magnifying glass and a couple of wicked-looking scalpels. As John joined him, Bright was examining the scalpels with a critical eye.

'Blunt as a rubber hammer,' he complained. 'No use at all.' He reached into an inside pocket, pulled out a wooden case and opened it to reveal three gleaming scalpels lying on a bed of velvet. 'Good job I brought my own.'

Ms Session shooed Terry McBride over to join John and Bright. Terry was protesting bitterly.

'Oh, *Miss*, do I have to?'

'Everyone else is in threes. *Somebody* has to work with him.'

John glanced at Bright, who seemed quite unconcerned. John sighed. It wasn't exactly that people disliked Bright; in fact, sometimes he was very popular, especially when people were choosing teams for football games. Bright could make a ball move any way he wanted, and could conjure up goals from seemingly impossible distances and angles.

In science classes, however, nobody wanted to work with Bright. His air of superiority got on everyone's nerves. Even John, who knew him better than anyone else, had to admit that listening to Bright getting carried away with his own cleverness made his teeth ache. Unfortunately, since Bright and John always worked together, nobody could work with John without having to work with Bright as well, so John shared Bright's unpopularity. Bright didn't seem to mind this, but John did.

Terry sat grumpily beside John, and Ms Session went back to the front of the class and tapped her knuckles on a chart showing a cutaway section of a kidney.

'Now,' she said briskly, 'the kidneys are organs found in the lower abdomen – roughly, in the small of the back. Their main job is to filter waste products out of the blood and store them as urine, which is later passed from the body.' There were a few snickers, instantly quelled by a withering look from Ms Session. 'Now, take your scalpels, and make a long incision *here* …'

All around the class, people prodded cautiously at their kidneys. Only Bright sliced confidently halfway through his kidney and then sat looking smug while others hacked away messily.

'If you look inside the incision you have just made,' said Ms Session, 'you'll see a lot of empty chambers. Together, these make up the renal pelvis, which is where the urine is collected.'

John felt cold sweat begin to break out on his forehead.

'Now, I want you to slice all the way through the kidney, cutting it in half. Then take a magnifying glass and draw what you can see.'

While Bright sliced expertly away and Terry leaned forward with the magnifying glass, John stared fixedly at the biology teacher. Her pupils had been delighted to find that Ms Session's first name was 'Vivienne'. 'Vivvy-Session', John thought grimly, was a particularly suitable name for somebody who was never happy unless her pupils were up to their elbows in gore.

'Is there something the matter, John?'

'No, Miss.' Steeling himself, John looked down at the oozing kidney which Bright had neatly cut in half. Taking a pencil in his shaking hand, he began to draw.

'There you are.' Bright was cleaning his scalpel and looking pleased with himself. He brushed one hand through his mass of spiky, untidy hair. 'It just

goes to show how important it is to look after your specimens. That is a perfectly healthy kidney.'

Terry looked up from the magnifying glass. 'But it's dead,' he objected.

Bright looked annoyed. 'Well, yes, it's *dead*, obviously it's dead, but apart from that it's perfectly healthy.' He gave John a disapproving look. 'I bet your kidneys don't look like that – not with all that Coke you drink, and stuffing your face with crisps every five minutes.' John stared goggle-eyed at the kidney in the dish as Terry prodded it with a scalpel. He felt the room begin to swim all around him.

'Anyway,' said Bright as Terry passed the magnifying glass over to John, who took it with some reluctance, 'when you say something's dead, all that means is that it's stopped working. You wouldn't call a car dead just because the engine wasn't running, would you?'

'Yeah,' said Terry, 'but the difference is, to get a car going again, all you've got to do is turn the key in the ignition, but if somebody dies, you can't just get them going again, can you?'

'Why not?' demanded Bright. 'There are all sorts of machines around these days to keep bits of the body going long after they would normally have stopped working.' He indicated the kidney. 'Dialysis machines for kidneys, life support machines for the lungs and the heart. You can even take a heart out of one person and put it in another.'

'Yeah, but …'

'Doctors can only declare that a person's dead if there's no electrical activity going on in their brain.' Bright glanced over at John and sniffed. 'Mind you, with some people they'd have to use some other test. People,' he added pointedly, 'whose brains show no sign of activity at all.'

John didn't rise to the bait. He was staring through the magnifying glass at microscopic horrors that made his eyes glaze over.

Ms Session tapped on her chart again for silence. 'Now, the outer layer of the kidney is called the cortex. Who can tell me what they can see in this layer?'

No hands went up. After several seconds, Bright raised an arm lazily. Ms Session looked at him coldly, but only said, 'Yes?'

'There are lots of small round structures called Bowman's capsules,' recited Bright in a bored voice. 'Each capsule contains looped blood vessels that make up the glomerulus. The capsule empties into the promaxial convoluted tubule ...'

Ms Session shook her head wearily. 'You can see all that, can you?'

Bright looked disdainful. 'Not with this silly little magnifying glass, no. It's not powerful enough. But I know it's there – it's in all the textbooks.'

Ms Session sighed. 'It must be terrible to know everything. Doesn't anything ever surprise you?'

Bright looked at her with amazement. He clearly didn't understand the question.

For the rest of the class, Ms Session pointed out features on the chart and the class tried to identify them in their kidneys. John felt as though his head was becoming detached from his body and floating gently away.

At last, Ms Session instructed the class to clear up and then called everyone around her bench at the front of the lab. Something was lying in the middle of the bench under a cover.

'Now, tomorrow,' she told them, 'we'll be looking at the heart and lungs.' She whipped the cover away. John gave a strangled whimper. He felt his knees go wobbly.

Sitting on the bench was a complete set of heart and lungs from some animal. John saw to his horror that a gristly tube from the lungs was connected to a set of bellows.

Ms Session picked up the bellows. 'So, when I see you again, we will be delving into the mysteries of respiration.'

She squeezed the bellows. The lungs on the bench inflated horribly as the bellows pumped air into them. In, out … in, out …

John's eyeballs rolled up in his head. He collapsed bonelessly to the floor in a dead faint.

CHAPTER TWO

Shells and Shelley

'What's the matter with you?' Bright demanded as he and John walked home from school. 'You see a tiny bit of body tissue and pass out!'

John had spent the whole day being teased about fainting in science, and he'd had enough. 'It wasn't a tiny bit,' he protested. 'It was a whole set of lungs.' He shuddered. 'And they moved.'

Bright gave him a pitying look. 'You could never be a surgeon, or a butcher, or a pathologist.'

'For your information, I don't want to be a surgeon or a butcher and I certainly don't want to murder people with an axe.'

Bright shook his head. 'That's a psychopath,' he said.

There was a pause.

'Right, of course it is. I knew that,' replied John unconvincingly.

There was a longer pause.

'What exactly is a pathologist?' John asked sheepishly.

'Someone who cuts up dead bodies and looks at their insides,' replied Bright with sadistic relish.

John began to feel queasy again.

Bright saw John's face turning pale and took pity on him. 'Come on, let's go to Dave's. There won't be any blood or body bits there.'

John wouldn't have bet on it. He'd been to David Thomas Vickers' Military Surplus Stores many times with Bright. It was better known as Dodgy Dave's and was the place where Bright acquired all sorts of interesting gadgets to help him in his experiments.

It wasn't called Dodgy Dave's for nothing. Dodgy Dave sold all sorts of ex-military equipment which, if it wasn't actually surplus to requirements right now, almost certainly would be, one day. The words 'legal' and 'Dodgy Dave' didn't really go together. So if there were a few bits of left-over body in a box lurking at the back of

Dave's yard, it wouldn't have surprised John in the slightest.

The two boys stepped through a gateway in a tatty board fence and into the scrapyard that was Dodgy Dave's. The yard never failed to amaze John. It was full of military hardware that Dave had somehow managed to 'get hold of': rockets, missiles, shells (with most of the dangerous bits taken out) and even an armoured car surrounded by camouflage nets, ammunition boxes and sandbags.

As Bright and John entered the steel building at the far end of the yard, they saw a figure dressed in full combat-gear, crouched over a small electronic screen. The screen gave off a green glow and occasionally emitted a high-pitched squeal.

Bright peered over the hunched figure and studied the electronic gizmo. After a few seconds, he grinned and nodded his head knowingly. He coughed. 'Is that one of those new rocket guidance systems that the Americans have been working on?'

Dodgy Dave shot up with the look of a startled rabbit.

'How can that be surplus?' continued Bright. 'It's only just been invented.'

'Hey, Vernie, my man! What a surprise!' Guilt was written all over Dave's face. It might have been possible to see fear in his eyes, except his eyes couldn't be seen. They were hidden under a pair of dark sunglasses. Dave liked to try and con people into believing he was an ex-American serviceman, a pose spoilt only by the fact that he'd been born in Luton. Now he whisked the beret he was wearing off his head and put it over the offending item. 'Heck, Vernie boy, a day is a long time in technology. What's new today is past its sell-by date tomorrow.'

'Hmm.' Bright looked deeply suspicious.

Dave looked around and dropped his voice to a conspiratorial whisper.

'Tell you what, you keep mum about the little thing here …' He nodded at his beret, '… and I'll scratch your back, know what I mean?'

'Well, I might want one or two things for my experiments in the near future … or maybe a small favour …' Bright left the suggestion hanging in the air.

'No problemo. Whatever you want. Just, er, just don't mention the out-of-date gizmo.' Dodgy Dave picked up his beret and the offending article and deposited them under a counter.

'Deal.' Bright nodded. He looked around the room. 'Anything new in, apart from the rocket thing?'

'I thought you said you wouldn't mention that!' hissed Dave.

'Only among friends,' Bright assured him.

Dave nodded towards a stack of ancient-looking green metal storage boxes. John could just make out US ARMY stencilled in white on their sides.

'There's a pile o' boxes there. Full of I-don't-know-what. Came in from some Yank company that just got decommissioned and sent back to the US of A. They been stationed out in Germany since double-u-double-u-two.'

John turned to Bright for a translation. 'World War Two,' Bright explained.

Dave's eyes glazed over. 'Yes, sir, that was a hell of a time. Sixth of June 1944. D-Day. Utah and Omaha beach. I remember it like it was yesterday. It wasn't pretty, boys, I can tell you …' Dave wandered over to a sandbag and began to stroke it nostalgically.

John glanced at Bright quizzically. 'That was over fifty years ago!' he whispered. 'He's not that old, is he?'

Bright shook his head. 'Mention a war and he's been in it. He even claims that he was at Waterloo!'

'The station?'

'The battle, you idiot. I think he gets a bit confused about reality.'

John gave Bright a quick look. Confused about reality? Talk about the pot calling the kettle black!

'Hey, Vernie!' Dave cried out. 'I just remembered! I also had a shipment of strange-

looking dials and boxes with wires and electrodes all hanging out.'

'What do they do?' asked Bright, suddenly interested.

'Gee, I don't know, I was hoping you'd be able to tell me. They're out the back ...'

Bright's eyes lit up. 'Show me!' he exclaimed and charged after Dave, leaving John standing on his own.

Typical Bright, thought John. Forget that I'm here. He's more interested in machines than people. John sighed and looked around. His gaze fell on the metal storage boxes. What had Dave said about them? 'Full of I-don't-know-what.'

John had an overwhelming urge to open them up and look inside. He wandered over to the boxes. He reached for the green metal clasps and stopped. What was he doing? There could be all sorts of dangerous and horrible things inside the boxes. For instance, bits of body …

Another gruesome thought struck John. What was the name of the box in Greek mythology that someone had opened and let out all kinds of bad things like disease and greed? John seemed to recall it sounded like some kind of animal. Panda's box? No, it wasn't that. It was …

'Pandora's box!' whispered John. That was it! What if these boxes were like Pandora's box, and by opening them, *he* let something bad out into the world?

But the urge to look inside the boxes was too great. Curiosity killed the cat, thought John. Ah well, meow!

Carefully, he flicked the first clasp back, then the second. He took a deep breath, slowly pushed the lid open …

… and breathed a sigh of relief. There were no kidneys, blood or gore, just some old papers and notebooks.

He began to rummage through the contents of the box. There were scrolls tied with ribbons, fading notebooks and dozens of yellowing pages with copperplate writing. They were certainly old. Probably antique.

John picked up a dusty notebook. A faded label on the front read 'Company museum collection. Box A.' John opened the book. It seemed to be a list of things in the collection. Very boring. He put it aside and dug deeper.

Underneath the layers of dust, John could make out a thicker book with a red leather cover and faded black writing. Maybe that would be more interesting. As he pulled it out of the box, a card fell out of it. He picked it up and read:

Item A24. Translation into English of a notebook found in bombed remains of a house in Ingolstadt, Germany – 8th October 1945

John wiped the dust from the book. He opened the brittle pages carefully, and began to read. As he did so, his insides began to tingle. He snapped the book shut again and stared at its cover for some seconds, trying to come to terms with what he was holding.

He read the title.

The Notebook of Victor Frankenstein
1815

John stared, open-mouthed. Frankenstein's notebook! Surely it couldn't be ... He flicked through the pages and started to feel light-headed. They were covered with sketches and drawings of body parts. Hearts, livers, kidneys, muscles, nerves, bones and skin were drawn in minute detail. There were notes as well. Pages and pages of them.

The sound of a door opening made John jump. He threw the book back into the box and slammed the lid shut.

Bright and Dave walked back into the room.

'Er, hi there, that was quick, did you find anything interesting?' gabbled John.

Bright gave him a sharp look. 'No. Did you?'

'No, of course not, why should I?' answered John, far too quickly. He felt himself going a guilty shade of red.

Bright eyed John suspiciously, but decided not to press the matter.

John smiled cheerily. 'Er, Dodg ... I mean, Dave, could I have one of those storage boxes?' he asked in his best innocent voice.

Bright raised an eyebrow.

'It'll be useful for storing my computer games,' explained John.

'Sure thing, dude,' said Dave, nodding. 'I haven't had time to look through them. Take it as seen?'

'OK.' John nodded enthusiastically. He pointed to the storage box with Frankenstein's notebook in. 'This one will do.'

Dave looked at the box. 'It's a bit scratched. Why don't you take a different one?'

'No, I want this one,' John insisted.

Bright raised another eyebrow.

Dave shrugged. 'Suit yourself. That'll be twenty big ones.'

There was a silence as John realized what Dave was asking. 'Twenty pounds!' he exclaimed. 'I haven't got twenty pounds.'

Dave shrugged. 'Sorry about that, but business

is business, dude.'

John's face dropped.

Bright's matter-of-fact cough broke the silence. 'Huh hum. It would be a terrible thing if certain persons found out about a certain out-of-date rocket guidance system ...'

Dodgy Dave frowned. 'You promised you wouldn't say anything.'

'I did.' Bright nodded at John. 'He didn't.'

In the blinking of an eye, Dave picked up the box and thrust it into John's hands. 'Tell you what, you can have it for free!'

'Thanks,' said John, smiling.

'Well, we must be going,' said Bright. 'Come on.'

As they waved their farewells to Dave, Bright hissed in John's ear, 'We'll go back to my lab and then you can tell me what you've discovered in that box that is so important.'

John stared wide-eyed at Bright. 'How do you know there's something important in the box?'

Bright tapped the side of his nose. 'Elementary, my dear Watt.'

John stood in Bright's kitchen as Bright went

through the security checks to get into the lab. Accepting his palm print and retina scan, the door clicked open. John shuffled through it. He lugged the box down a flight of concrete steps into the cellar that served as Bright's laboratory, and dumped it on a workbench.

As Bright clattered down the steps behind him John automatically peered into Horace's cage. Horace was Bright's laboratory guinea pig. John had saved Horace from one of Bright's experiments, and though Bright had promised never to harm Horace, John felt responsible for checking that he was sticking to his word.

'Hello, Horace,' he said. The guinea pig gave him a disapproving look and carried on chewing a cabbage leaf.

Bright rubbed his hands together briskly. 'Where is it then?'

John opened the box and took out the notebook. He handed it to Bright.

Bright had been dubious when John told him about the notebook on the way home. But now, as he flicked through a few pages, his eyes lit up and a smile began to spread across his face. 'Incredible!' he whispered. 'Unbelievable!'

'But it's got to be a fake,' said John. 'Frankenstein didn't really exist. Anyway, he was a monster, so he couldn't have written anything down.'

'Wrong!' announced Bright. 'Frankenstein was the name of the person who created the monster. Victor Frankenstein.'

'Anyway, he still wasn't real. He was a character in a book.'

Bright switched his computer on. 'We need information. Let's go surfing …'

After a couple of minutes on the Net, they found what they were looking for.

'Here it is,' squeaked John as he peered at the screen and began to read. '"*Frankenstein* was written by Mary Shelley in Switzerland in 1818. It is the story of Victor Frankenstein, a student who discovers the secret of life. He creates a creature from bits of bodies that he collects from graveyards and hospitals …"' John took a deep breath and tried not to think about dozens of body bits being sewn together. '"But Frankenstein's creation turns into a monster that is responsible for several deaths. It is a moral story about tampering with nature."'

'Hmm,' snorted Bright. 'Typical. Nature is there

to be improved.' He picked up the notebook.

'Where did you say this book was found?' he asked, a few minutes later.

John frowned with the effort of memory. 'The card said "Ingo" something.'

'Ingolstadt.' Bright held the book up and pointed out a passage for John to read …

> *Today I am leaving my home in Geneva for a new life as a student at the University of Ingolstadt …*

'Well, OK,' said John dubiously, 'but that doesn't prove …'

'Sshhh!' Bright read on. After a while he gave a soft whistle. Peering over his shoulder, John read:

> *… in the midst of this darkness, a sudden light broke in upon me — a light so brilliant and wondrous, yet so simple. After days and nights of incredible labour and fatigue, I succeeded in discovering the cause of generation and life; nay, more, I became myself capable of bestowing animation upon lifeless matter.*

'The secret of life,' whispered Bright.

John shook his head stubbornly. 'It's only a story!'

Bright swung round to face him. 'What if Frankenstein was a real person, but what he did was so terrible that he had to disguise it as fiction ...?'

'Oh, come on,' protested John.

'... and he met Mary Shelley and they came to an agreement that she could write up his story as a novel ...?' Bright had a wild look in his eye. John had seen it before – when Bright's experiments were getting interesting.

'Just leave the notebook with me,' Bright said casually. 'I'll get my dad to run some tests on it to see if it's authentic.'

John wasn't sure. 'You're not having any strange ideas, are you?'

Bright looked hurt. 'Strange ideas, me? Never!'

John's gaze shifted to Horace. 'Remember you promised not to experiment on any living things.'

Bright looked hurt. 'I know I did.' He held up his hand. 'I, Vernon Bright, promise once again, not to experiment on any living things.'

John nodded. For all his faults, Bright was a person who kept a promise. 'All right, you can keep it,' said John. He wagged a stern finger at Bright. 'No living things.'

The Notebook
of
Victor Frankenstein
1815

'No living things, I promise.' A grin broke slowly across Bright's face. 'Quite the reverse in fact.'

Two hours later, John was lying on his bed. He was feeling unwell. When he'd arrived home his mother had moaned about him being late and then banged down his evening meal in front of him. Steak and kidney pie.

John had been saved from fainting by the fact

27

that he was violently sick instead. His mum had sent him up to bed and he now lay there recuperating and thinking.

Why were bodies such complicated things? Made up of so many different parts, all joined together in an incredible design. Amazing when you thought about it!

His thoughts drifted to the notebook. What if Bright was right, and Frankenstein was a real person? What if he really had discovered the secret of life and written it all down in the notebook? John began to feel a little concerned. What would Bright do with such information? He shook his head and reassured himself with the thought that Bright had promised not to experiment on any living things.

'No living things, I promise. Quite the reverse.'

'Quite the reverse!' John sat bolt upright.

Bright hadn't mentioned anything about experimenting on things that were dead!

CHAPTER THREE

Happy Landings!

'What you said yesterday …' John faltered.

Bright raised an eyebrow in his direction.

'You know, about not doing experiments on living things, doing the opposite …? Does that mean what I think it does? Because if it does … I mean, you couldn't … you *wouldn't* …' John's voice dropped to a whisper. 'You shouldn't …'

They were waiting outside the gym for their PE class. John hopped from one foot to the other with anxiety while Bright eyed him coolly.

'I wish you'd just relax,' Bright drawled. 'What's the matter with you? Haven't you got any scientific curiosity?'

'Not when it comes to mucking about with dead

29

bodies, no!' John's imagination was running on turbo, conjuring up images of dreadful zombies that rose from their graves and came shambling towards him and Bright, full of maggots and attitude. 'That's a sure way to get Things with eyes like raw liver coming after you and ripping your head off!'

'Why would they do that?'

'So they can carry it around in a bag until your brain turns to jelly and then suck it out through your nostrils.'

Bright gave him a disgusted look. 'You watch too many horror movies. There are no such things as ... er ... Things.'

'That's what everyone says until they wind up with their head in a holdall!'

'Anyway, my experiments are purely theoretical.'

'You try telling some creepy undead weirdo he's purely theoretical while he's sucking your brains through your nose!'

'Will you get a grip?' Bright looked pained. 'I'm not going to start experimenting on dead people! What do you think I am?'

John couldn't think of a polite answer to this question, so he said nothing.

'That's where Frankenstein went wrong, you see. It's all there in the notebook. He just couldn't wait. Always rushing into things – no scientific method. You can't expect to make a person out of bits without doing a lot of basic experimentation first. Human beings are very complicated. If I was going to try anything like that ...' Bright held up a hand as John opened his mouth to protest, 'I said *if* – I'd want to start on something – well – a lot simpler.'

John gave him a suspicious look. 'What do you mean, a lot simpler?' he asked.

Bright was saved from having to reply by the arrival of their teacher for the PE session.

Mr Hardman had joined the school in September. He had been in the Royal Marines until (according to school rumour) he'd been thrown out for cruelty, and decided to retrain as a PE teacher. He had a bullet head with short ginger hair like peach fuzz, a hatchet jaw and no neck. His massive chest made his waist and legs look tiny, giving him the general shape of an ice-cream cone. He had two small, but unpleasant, tattoos. He ironed his T-shirts and his tracksuit bottoms. He loathed Vernon Bright because Bright never 'made an effort'.

During football matches, Bright would hardly break into a trot, but every pass he made was perfect and he seemed able to score goals at will. In Mr Hardman's book (which, Bright remarked to John, must be a very thin book with short words and big pictures), victory on the football pitch should be gained only through blood, sweat and tears. The idea that you could win by being more skilful than the other side was torment to his soul. It was the sort of thing sneaky foreigners did. It just wasn't playing the game.

Today's lesson was in the gym. The class piled into the echoing room with its smells of sweat and floor polish.

'Right,' snarled Mr Hardman (who snarled everything), 'today I am going to teach you the principles of unarmed combat.' There were a few groans. Mr Hardman's icy blue eyes swept over the group. 'What you learn today is for your personal safety, so pay attention!'

For the next few minutes, Mr Hardman taught his pupils how to gouge an attacker's eyes out, dislocate his thumbs, crush his throat with a blow from the elbow, and knee him in places that it made John's eyes water just to think about. As Mr Hardman demonstrated these blood-curdling moves on trembling students, Bright leaned against the wall-bars with folded arms, watching the proceedings with disdain. Occasionally, Mr Hardman glanced in his direction. Every time he did so, the veins on his forehead pulsed.

Eventually, he turned to Bright with a leer.

'I hope I haven't been boring you,' he rasped.

'Not at all,' Bright said in a nearly polite voice that made Mr Hardman's veins turn a funny colour. 'I'm sure many of those moves would be very effective. Primitive, but effective.'

'Oh. Is that right?' Mr Hardman thrust his chin out. 'Well, laddie, if you're so clever, perhaps you'd like to show the rest of us how to deal with an unprovoked attack?'

Bright shrugged carelessly. 'If you like.' He moved away from the wall-bars and stood facing Mr Hardman, looking as relaxed as it's possible to get without falling over.

The silly nit, John thought. He's done it this time. Hardman'll murder him.

The PE teacher stood a few paces away from Bright. 'Now, let's see what you've learnt. I'm going to come at you; you defend yourself. I promise I won't hurt you,' he grinned malevolently at Bright, 'much.'

Bright picked a microscopic piece of fluff from his T-shirt. 'Whatever you say.'

John bit his lip and half-closed his eyes.

With a snarl, Mr Hardman launched himself at Bright. There was a blur of movement. John blinked. Bright had stepped to one side and swatted Mr Hardman's clutching arms away as casually as if he were dealing with an annoying fly.

The teacher spun back to face Bright. A

dangerous light gleamed in his eyes. He dropped into a Ninja crouch.

'Haaaiiiiioooooouuuuuwuwwuwwuwwwwww!'

John gulped. The ex-marine had clearly lost it. Bright watched impassively as their instructor executed a terrifying series of bone-crunching karate chops, before giving another terrifying scream of rage and launching a flying drop-kick at his tormentor.

John covered his face with his hands – which was a pity, as he missed the dexterous sidestep and twist with which Bright sent the astonished martial arts expert flying, upside down, into the wall-bars.

There was a horrendous crash and the crack of splitting timber.

Cautiously, Mr Hardman's students approached his groaning, half-conscious body.

'What a doofus,' someone said.

'I wouldn't call him a doofus,' someone else argued, 'I'd call him a dipstick. What would you call him, Bright?'

Bright eyed the remains. 'Right now,' he said thoughtfully, 'I'd call him an ambulance.'

'It's called Akido,' Bright explained to John ten minutes later as they got changed. 'Of course, it's related to Judo and other forms of self defence, but in one way it's different from every other form of martial art.'

'Really? And how is it ...?'

'It uses scientific principles.'

Of course, John thought.

'Moments of force, things like that. In Akido, what you aim to do is to turn an opponent's strength against himself. The more force he uses in attacking you, the more force you have to defend yourself.'

'So,' said John slowly, 'it only works if someone actually attacks you?'

Bright looked pleased. 'That's right. You can't

use it for attack – it just doesn't work that way. You can only use it for defence. But as a defence it's practically unbeatable.' He grinned. 'The bigger they are, the harder they fall.'

John had been dreading the final biology class of the term. He had come in for a lot of 'funny' remarks about passing out the day before ('What's worse, a wuss or a Watt?'), and didn't want to give his tormentors any more ammunition.

However, Ms Session seemed to have been rattled by John's collapse. In this lesson she contented herself with showing slides and charts of the heart and lungs, so that the class could fill in a worksheet of notes and diagrams. John found it much easier to deal with drawings of hearts and lungs than the flesh and blood – especially the blood – of the real thing. Bright, on the other hand, gave a contemptuous sniff when he saw what they had to do, completed his worksheet in the first ten minutes, and spent the rest of the lesson reading a book called *Advanced Molecular Biology*.

As the class packed away, Ms Session rapped her board duster on the bench to get everyone's attention. 'All right.' She glared at people who were still fumbling with their bags and waited for silence. 'This is our last class before the Christmas break,' she went on, 'so who is going to have the pleasure of Mister Nibbles' company over the holidays?'

Bright immediately put his hand up. 'I will,' he said.

Ms Session gave him a very hard look. 'You will not!' she said.

John glanced at the corner of the lab where Mister Nibbles, the science lab hamster, was determinedly stuffing food from his dish into his cheek pouches and carrying it to his nest for safekeeping. Propped up behind his cage was a dusty maze that Ms Session occasionally tried to use for experiments in animal behaviour. As Mister Nibbles promptly curled up and went to sleep every time he was put in it, its educational value, and that of Mister Nibbles himself, wasn't very clear. Even so, Ms Session was obviously not keen on the idea of Mister Nibbles spending the Christmas holidays with Vernon Bright.

Bright was the picture of injured innocence. 'I wouldn't do anything to it!'

'Oh no?' Ms Session gave a snort of disbelief.

'What about the rat you took home last Christmas? For the next six months, we had to put fresh newspaper in his cage every day ...'

'But all animals are supposed to have fresh newspaper in their cages every day,' objected Bright.

'Yes, but not to *read*. And what about the school tortoise?'

Bright sat stony-faced. John gave him a playful nudge. 'What did you do, put wheels on it? Ha ha ... ha ...' He tailed off as he caught the look in Bright's eye. 'It was just a joke,' he said weakly. 'You didn't really, did you?'

'There's nothing wrong with that tortoise,' Bright said indignantly. 'It's perfectly fit and healthy.'

'You may be right, but nobody knows for sure, do they?' snapped Ms Session. 'Nobody's been able to catch it yet!'

Bright shrugged. 'There you are then.'

Ms Session continued to glare at Bright while the rest of the class looked at each other and shuffled their feet. Most of them had had inquisitive fingers bitten by Mister Nibbles at some time or other, and they weren't too keen on the idea of having the hamster as a Christmas house guest.

Eventually, John's hand went up. 'I'll take him, Miss.'

Ms Session gave him a long, hard look before replying.

'Very well. Come and see me after school on Friday and I'll have his cage ready. But let me be absolutely clear about one thing.' She pointed a stern finger at John. 'This poor animal is to stay at your house over Christmas. It is not, under any circumstances, to find its way into Vernon Bright's house. If Vernon Bright comes to visit you in your home, he is not to be left in a room alone with Mister Nibbles, even for a few minutes. I shall hold you personally responsible for the safety of this hamster, and the first rule you will follow in keeping it safe is this ...' Ms Session pointed accusingly at Bright and her voice quavered with emotion, 'never let Vernon Bright anywhere near it!'

The rest of the week passed quietly enough. The Deputy Principal had got very hot under the collar about the incident in the gym. However, the whole class had insisted that Bright had only done what Mr Hardman told him to do. Mr Hardman himself had agreed (through gritted teeth) that the whole thing had just been an unlucky accident and the worst that Bright had suffered was a warning to 'be more careful in future'.

Snow began to fall on Friday morning, leaving the school grounds looking like a badly iced Christmas cake (minus the plastic Santa and reindeers). The streets around the school were soon covered in a treacherous, white, icy glaze and streetlights flickered on in a futile attempt to pierce the growing darkness.

Amongst the pupils there was an excited anticipation of forthcoming snowball fights. Teachers, however, looked out miserably at the falling flakes and grumbled that the Head should shut the school immediately, otherwise how on earth would they be able to get home in this weather?

Eventually, a note came round to say the school would close for the end of term at lunchtime. This announcement was greeted with cheers, and when the final bell of the day rang, there was a mad scramble to get outdoors: kids dashed outside to make snowballs, and teachers hurried out to rescue their snow-covered cars and avoid the white missiles that were now peppering the air.

Having collected Mister Nibbles for his winter vacation, John headed across the playground, threading his way through a snowball crossfire.

'Hi, Bright!' John slithered over to where Bright was laying down a deadly accurate artillery barrage in a free-for-all twenty-a-side snowball fight. 'I've got Mister Nibbles – d'you want to help me carry him home?'

Bright gave him a haughty glance. 'Didn't you hear Ms Session? I'm not allowed anywhere near Mister Nibbles. I'm not to be trusted.' He turned his back on John.

Sighing, John hoisted the cage into a slightly more comfortable position and set off on the long walk home.

John pushed the back door of his house open with his bottom and backed into the kitchen.

'Hidearhaveagooddayatschool?' breezed his mum.

'No, my leg dropped off, the school was burnt down and I got suspended for poisoning the Head.'

'Did you, dear? Oh good.'

John sighed. Did his mum *ever* listen to him?

As he put the hamster cage down on the kitchen table, John felt something rub against his leg. It was Gorgeous, the family cat. 'Hello, Gorgeous,' he said and felt silly. What a stupid name for a cat, he thought. Another one of his mum's great ideas.

She'd adopted a cat from the RSPCA when she and John had moved into the house six months ago: 'To keep us both company, now that your father's left.'

It had been a bad time when his parents split up. John and his mother had moved to a new town, 'for a new start' as she put it. Luckily, John had settled down pretty quickly. He'd met Vernon Bright on his first day at Elmley. Since then he'd grown to tolerate his new school and the time he spent with Bright was always interesting, to say the least.

Still, John didn't think it was much of an exchange, swapping his dad for a mangy-looking brown and white cat that did nothing but eat, sleep and bring in dead birds that it had 'hunted' down.

Gorgeous meowed back at John, leapt up on to the kitchen table with a single bound and started eyeing Mister Nibbles with an evil glint in his eyes.

'Don't even think about it,' ordered John as he swatted the cat from the table. 'Mister Nibbles is under my protection!'

'What's that?' His mother pointed at Mister Nibbles' cage.

'Our school hamster. I offered to look after him over the holiday.' John caught a look in his mum's eye. 'I didn't think you'd mind,' he said quickly. 'I thought it would be a bit of company over Christmas ...' John let the implication hang in the air.

His mum nodded an OK and John grinned to himself. He knew exactly how to get round her.

'Talking of company,' his mum said, 'I've got to look after Lulu for a bit.'

'Oh no!' protested John. 'Do you have to?' Lulu lived next door. Although she was only seven, she was all teeth, blonde curls and sulks. The phrase 'spoilt brat' had been invented for her.

'Don't make it into a problem, John. It's only for an hour or so. Anyway,' John's mother shot him a stare, 'it'll be a bit of company.'

John narrowed his eyes. Touché, he thought.

The doorbell rang. John's mother went to answer it while he took his chance to escape upstairs to the Lulu-Free-Zone safety of his bedroom. Sitting on his bed, John glanced at the list of instructions Ms Session had given him in order to ensure Mister Nibbles' well-being. At the bottom of the page she had scrawled in red ink:

'_DO NOT_ LET VERNON BRIGHT
NEAR MISTER NIBBLES!
OR ELSE ...!'

John wondered what the 'OR ELSE ...!' meant. He slipped the note into his pocket, feeling suddenly queasy as images of his own internal body parts having nasty things done to them sprang into his mind.

After an hour with his computer, during which he saved the universe, won the FA Cup and became world motor racing champion, John was just about to win an Olympic Gold medal when he was distracted by a shout from his mother.

'You can come down now. I'm taking Lulu home. Then I'm off to a meeting. Get yourself some food.'

John waited until the front door had shut and let out a huge sigh of relief. He switched off his computer and wandered downstairs.

As he entered the kitchen a nagging feeling hit him. He couldn't quite work out what it was. He looked around the kitchen. Something wasn't as it should be. Suddenly, an icy chill gripped his heart. Panic gushed through his whole body in a single heartbeat. He began to feel sick and his legs turned to blancmange.

Mister Nibbles' cage door was open!

John rushed over to the cage and began poking around the sawdust and shavings. The hamster wasn't there! In desperation, he picked the cage up and began to shake it.

With a flash of insight, he realized what had happened. Lulu must have been playing with the hamster and left the door open!

Out of the corner of his eye, John saw the flicker of a brown and white tail. He spun round. Gorgeous stopped dead in his tracks. If a cat could ever look guilty, Gorgeous had that look.

'Where's Mister Nibbles?!' screamed John.

The cat eyed him and, as if reading his mind, glanced towards a corner of the kitchen.

John saw a small furry ball moving in the corner.

He rushed towards it. But he was too slow. He felt a whoosh of air as Gorgeous sprang past him and picked up Mister Nibbles with one snap of his jaws.

'No!' yelled John. 'Drop him!'

Gorgeous headed for the cat flap, and shot through without touching the sides. John made a despairing dive and, unable to stop, slammed into the door. His head shot through the cat flap. Struggling to free himself, John watched the cat gallop along the garden path and disappear round the side of the house.

'Come back!' screamed John. With a desperate yank, he pulled the cat flap clean out of the door panel, and staggered to his feet, wearing it round his neck. He pulled frantically at the door handle.

'Gorgeous! Gorgeous!' John ran into the garden. 'Gorgeous!' He raced round to the front garden, trying to make out the cat's footprints in the snow. There they were! They led through the front gate. John pelted out of the garden and frantically looked up and down the street. Neither Gorgeous, nor Mister Nibbles, were anywhere to be seen. There were no more pawprints either.

'Come here, Gorgeous!' yelled John. A passing woman gave him a very funny look. He grabbed her arm. 'Have you seen a cat with a hamster in its mouth?'

The woman let fly with an intercontinental ballistic handbag, which caught John on the ear and sent him sprawling. As she hurried away, John caught sight of a brown blur as Gorgeous shot through a gap in the hedge and back into the garden. Cursing, and holding his throbbing ear, John followed, just in time to see the cat, with Mister Nibbles hanging limply from its mouth, disappear behind the garage.

Frantically, John pushed his way through the narrow gap between the garage and the back wall. There was a ripping noise as a nail tore a hole in his school trousers. John gritted his teeth and wriggled on. He had to get to the cat before …

'Mrrow.' The sound of a muffled meow above him made John look up. Somehow, Gorgeous had managed to get on top of the garage. He still had Mister Nibbles in his mouth. John thought he saw the hamster's paw twitch.

Hope gave him renewed strength. He scrambled up on to the back wall, and very carefully hauled himself up on to the ridge of the snow-covered garage roof. Gorgeous eyed him suspiciously.

Hardly breathing, and balancing precariously on the top of the sloping roof, John brought his other foot across the gap. 'Come here, Gorgeous,' he murmured, inching along the roof. 'Put the hamster down and keep your paws where I can see them.' Gorgeous backed away warily.

'Gotcha!' He made a sudden lunge at the cat, which skipped nimbly away. John gave a roar of fright as his feet went from under him. He landed face-first on the garage roof with a thump, and rolled uncontrollably down the steep slope.

Fortunately, a bush broke his fall.

Unfortunately, it was a holly bush.

As John lay groaning in the snow, he turned his head. Lying almost within reach of his outstretched hand was a tiny heap of fur. John rolled over towards it, reached out to pick it up …

And felt sick.

Mister Nibbles lay lifeless in the snow.

The hamster's fur was matted with blood. Tears began to stream down John's face. He suddenly felt very lonely and very scared. Ms Session would kill him! What should he do? Who could he turn to?